THE
TIME MACHINE
NEXT DOOR

RULE BREAKERS AND KIWI KEEPERS

Sunil lives next door to an amazing inventor – Alex. She has harnessed the power of boredom to slow time down, stop it and put it in reverse. They use her time machine – the Boring Machine – to explore the past. But things don't always go smoothly…

THE TIME MACHINE NEXT DOOR

RULE BREAKERS AND KIWI KEEPERS

ILLUSTRATED BY
REBECCA BAGLEY

ISZI LAWRENCE

BLOOMSBURY EDUCATION
LONDON OXFORD NEW YORK NEW DELHI SYDNEY

BLOOMSBURY EDUCATION

Bloomsbury Publishing Plc

50 Bedford Square, London, WC1B 3DP, UK

29 Earlsfort Terrace, Dublin 2, Ireland

BLOOMSBURY, BLOOMSBURY EDUCATION and the Diana logo are trademarks of
Bloomsbury Publishing Plc

First published in Great Britain in 2024 by Bloomsbury Publishing Plc

A catalogue record for this book is available from the British Library

ISBN: PB: 978-1-80199-116-2; ePDF: 978-1-80199-114-8; ePub: 978-1-80199-115-5

2 4 6 8 10 9 7 5 3 1

Text design by Amanda Carroll

Printed and bound by CPI Group (UK) Ltd, Croydon, CR0 4YY

To find out more about our authors and books visit www.bloomsbury.com and sign up
for our newsletters

CONTENTS

For Roslyn

CHAPTER ONE

Sunil looked at the paper.

'Which of these fractions is largest?' he read.

A **cold** feeling settled somewhere near his navel. He knew this. He'd done fractions hundreds of times.

Everyone else was bent over their classroom tables, writing furiously. Sunil was stuck on the first question. The easy one. Why hadn't he read the homework notes Miss Cook had sent home? He'd been sick all last week, and today was his first day back.

He swallowed. The answer should be obvious. Two was bigger than one but five was bigger than two. He couldn't remember if the number on top or underneath of the line was the denominator. He couldn't think. He had always thought he was good at maths. It made up for his bad spelling and inability to draw well. Now he wasn't good at anything. He was so **stupid**.

A wet mark suddenly landed

next to the question. Sunil sniffed. Oh no. He was **crying**. He looked around at the heads bent low over the classroom tables and at Miss Cook, marking something at the front of the room. His face was hot; he didn't want anyone to see. Had they noticed? More tears leaked out from behind his eyes. Oh no, no, no! Sunil made a break for it and **ran** to the door of the classroom.

'Sunil?'

Miss Cook looked up to see

Sunil push through the door.

'Sorry-I-really-need-the-toilet...'

He thought he heard his classmates laugh. He ran down the empty corridor to the boys' bathroom and shut himself in a stall. Why was he such a loser? Crying over a stupid maths test! What was wrong with him?

The door to the bathroom opened. Footsteps approached Sunil's hiding place and someone pushed on the stall door.

'Sunil?' It was Adam's voice. Sunil didn't like Adam.

'Go away!'

'Are you **crying**?' Adam chuckled. 'Aw, little baby Sunil.'

'Leave me alone!' Sunil said angrily.

'He's in here, miss!' Adam called.

More footsteps and a gentle tap on the stall door. 'Sunil? Are you alright?'

'I'm sick!' Sunil blurted. He made a pretend retching noise and spat into the empty toilet bowl.

'Open the door, dear,' Miss Cook said.

Sunil wiped his eyes with some paper and flushed the toilet. He opened the door and looked up at Miss Cook's concerned face.

'Were you sick?' she asked, touching his forehead. 'You are still a bit clammy and your eyes are all puffy.'

Sunil looked at Adam who made a pretend crying face. It was humiliating.

Mrs Cook said, 'Adam, please ask Ms Bakali to bring Sunil's bag to sick bay and sit with him until his parents come.'

Adam managed to pull another mock crying face before doing as he was told.

Sunil walked to sick bay with the teaching assistant, Ms Bakali. He felt terrible. He had lied. He wasn't sick; he just didn't want people to think he'd cried. Now he was being sent home.

His lie felt even worse because everyone was being so nice to him. Even his dad, who had stopped halfway through clearing out the attic to pick him up, didn't complain.

'Mum said she didn't think you'd fully recovered,' Dad said as he drove the car through the drizzle back to their house. 'Good thing

I was at home sorting through those boxes. I've found loads of old gadgets up in the loft. I must get Alex to look at them, sometime.'

Sunil nodded and watched the drops of rain sliding down the window. He didn't feel poorly. He felt like a fraud. He wasn't sick. He was just **really bad** at maths.

'What are you doing?' his dad asked when they got back to the house.

'I was just getting my things

ready for tonight,' Sunil said, grabbing his batting gloves from under the stairs.

'You're ill. You can't go to cricket practice!'

'But I feel fine!' said Sunil.

'You were sent home from school! You can't play sport. Go to bed.'

Sunil's heart broke. This would be the second week in a row he would have to miss practice. He picked up Tara the dog's old

tennis ball and squeezed it silently. Another week falling behind. He could be chucked off the team. All because he lied about being sick.

'Come on,' his dad said. 'I'll bring you some water.'

Sunil went upstairs and flopped face down on his bed. He wished he could go back and change everything. If only he hadn't pretended to be sick, or run to the bathroom, or if only he had read his homework. If only Miss Cook

hadn't done the test. Then he'd have had a normal day at school and this evening he would be going to cricket practice.

'I'm going to ask Auntie Alex to babysit this evening,' his dad said, placing a glass of water on the windowsill. 'That way your mother and I can still go out when you were supposed to be at cricket practice.'

Alex... it was like a switch flicked in Sunil's mind. He could change everything. Alex had a

time machine! All he had to do was travel back in time to morning break, sneak into the classroom and hide the maths tests. It was simple!

'Okay, Dad,' Sunil said, secretly grinning to himself that soon he would make everything better.

CHAPTER TWO

'No,' said Alex.

'What do you mean, "**no**"?!'
Sunil whined. 'I just want to use the
Boring Machine to go back in time
and hide the tests.'

'The Boring Machine isn't a
toy. Time travel is dangerous,' Alex
said. 'Particularly when the time

machine in question is powered by something as volatile as boredom.'

Sunil didn't know what volatile meant.[1] 'But don't you see? If I went back and hid the tests, I wouldn't have to pretend to be ill or miss cricket practice.'

1. If something is volatile it is unstable and unpredictable. In this case, something boring can easily turn out to be quite interesting. If the Boring Machine uses boredom to keep you in the past, but finds itself getting interested you could be yanked back into the future at any moment. Also, there is nothing to stop you being hurt or killed in the past, which is far more likely to happen if you land next to someone and frighten them.

'Firstly, you can't change the past,' Alex said, plopping herself down on the end of his bed. 'And B, you already know how dangerous the Boring Machine can be.'

'But…' Sunil felt tears come into his eyes again.

'And number 4,' Alex said, 'you're ill.'

'I only pretended to be sick so I didn't have to take the test!' Sunil explained.

'Sunil, you're nearly **crying**,' Alex pointed out.

'I am not!'

'It's okay. It's good to cry, otherwise your eyes get all dusty,' she said.[2] 'But it's also a sign that you're overtired. So get some sleep while I go downstairs and do some

2. Crying when you are sad is very healthy. Trying to stop yourself from crying is like trying to stop yourself sneezing. You can do it, but it will likely damage your insides.

experiments on your dad's old VHS player.'[3]

3. VHS means Video Home System. Before the internet allowed you to stream or download films and TV shows, people would rent or buy VHS cassettes from shops. They looked like thick books and were made of plastic with a magnetic tape spooled inside that contained the movie. One edge flipped up so the machine you fed it into could read the tape. Each cassette had adverts for other films or shows, which you had to watch or fast forward through. There was no menu and you couldn't jump to later parts of the tape. After the adverts it played the film or show you wanted to watch. You could also record live TV onto VHS tapes.

Sunil was **furious**. He had thought Alex was his friend but she wouldn't help him. He didn't need her stupid machine to travel back in time anyway, he thought. He knew that the Boring Machine used the power of boredom to send you back into the past.

All he had to do was bore himself to slow time down, stop and reverse it. Then he could go back to school, hide the tests and change history!

Sunil squeezed past the ladder going up into the attic and grabbed his dad's alarm clock from his parents' bedroom. He hurried back and placed the clock on the end of his bed. He sat as still as possible, staring at its plain white face. He tried to block out the faint tapping sound, and occasional buzz as Alex's experiments caused the lights to dim. He watched the second hand slowly tick around. It certainly seemed to be getting slower. Then

it happened. The second hand stopped, just above the number 3. Sunil felt a rush of excitement... and it started ticking again.

Sunil swore under his breath. If he couldn't do it without the machine, he would just have to sneak next door and use it anyway!

That... might be tricky. Alex locked her house because she was a responsible adult (and if her worms escaped again, she couldn't be sure they wouldn't get out into

the road like last time). Sunil knew
she had dozens of keys hanging
from the carabiner on her belt but
he couldn't just take them without
her noticing. Sunil looked out of his
bedroom window. It faced Alex's
frosted bathroom window which
had been stuck wide open ever since
she tried to make homemade glue
in the bathtub.

He went back onto the landing.
There was a faint **drilling** noise
coming from downstairs where

Alex was doing experiments on Dad's old gadgets. Sunil took the ladder down from the hatch up to the attic. It **clattered** noisily. He paused, waiting for Alex to stop and ask what he was up to, but the **drilling** carried on. The ladder was heavy and cumbersome. He knocked over his bedroom chair and left a couple of marks on the wall. Panting, he opened his window and, using all his strength, he slid the ladder across the gap between the houses. He nearly

dropped it as it **teetered** out of his window; it took all his strength to lift it level and slide the far end into Alex's bathroom.

Sunil didn't allow himself time to think about what would happen if he fell. He immediately got onto the ladder and started walking between the houses. He had only taken two steps before a gust of wind made him nervous. The ground seemed to rise up and down like waves so he hunched down, clinging to the sides of the ladder

and
breathing
hard through
his nose. He
focused his gaze
on Alex's bathroom window and
slowly began to crawl. The ladder
shook a little from side to side but
he kept going and, once he got to the

window, he
scrambled
inside. To his
horror, just as his
foot left the ladder,
it suddenly fell, crashing down onto
the fence between the two houses.

If he had still been on it... but
he had no time to think about the

crunch his bones would have made hitting the ground.[4] He had to be quick. Alex would have heard the **smash** and gone outside to check what was going on. It wouldn't take her long to realise what he'd done. He jumped down off the windowsill onto the bathtub full of solid glue, and ran out of Alex's bathroom.

4. I'm sure you don't need me to tell you that this was a really terrible and dangerous idea which a) Sunil should never have tried and b) no one else should ever try either.

Chapter Three

To Sunil's surprise, Wiki, Mr
Shaykes's trained kiwi, stood at
the bottom of the stairs, **peeping**
furiously. This startled Sunil.
Why did Alex have the ruthless
entrepreneur's sniffer-bird in her

house?[1] Was Mr Shaykes here? He was always trying to find ways to take advantage of Sunil, Alex or the Boring Machine for one of his hair-brained business ideas.

'Mr Shaykes?' Sunil called, but there was no response other than the snarling of the angry kiwi at his feet. He looked down at the bird. 'What are you doing here?'

1. Kiwis have an excellent sense of smell. Their nostrils are on the tip of their long beaks so they can snuffle out bugs in leaf litter. Previously Wiki had been trained to smell for interesting objects – see *The Time Machine Next Door: Explorers and Milkshakes* for more details.

The bird huffed, blocking his route.

'Here.' Sunil took Tara's tennis ball out of his pocket and threw it towards the tank in Alex's living room where her pet lobster lived.

'Fetch.'

Wiki immediately chased after it. Not wanting to waste time, Sunil opened the door to the downstairs

toilet where the Boring Machine was kept and, after moving the mega pack of toilet paper out of the way, pressed the 'on' button. It *whirred* and **clunked** and then the screen went from dark to pale blue.

'The ancient Egyptian empire lasted so long, there were ancient Egyptian archaeologists studying ancient Egypt,' it said.

'That's a good fact, BM,' Sunil

said. 'Has Alex programmed you to tell her better ones?'

'Ah, Sunil, where are we going today?' the Boring Machine purred.

'I need to get to my school around lunchtime today,' Sunil explained. 'Do you have enough power?'

'Affirmative! I'm full of pictures of breakfasts posted on social media.'

The Boring Machine used the most mind-numbing things possible to create the boredom to power itself. Boredom slowed time down and reversed it. However, it could only keep you in the past as long as it had enough boredom power to hold you there.

'I require an artefact,' the BM said.

The Boring Machine used an object to pinpoint a place in time to send you to. You could only go

where that object had been. Which
meant Sunil needed something that
had been at school with him that
day.

'Here.' Sunil took off his hoodie
and placed it into the Boring
Machine's artefact drawer. 'Will
that do?'

It *whirred* and **clicked** and *whirred*
some more.

'You've got to hurry!' Sunil
heard Alex's keys in the front door.

'Warning. Jamming error,' the machine said. 'Do you wish to proceed?'

Sunil heard the front door **crash** open. Alex was home!

'Just go now!' he said, grabbing the handles.

'Sunil?'

Sunil heard Alex's voice but she was too late. She had only just opened the door to the downstairs toilet before he felt himself **flip** backwards into the past.

Chapter Four

'I'm going to hit you!'

It was warm. The ground was hot in a way that it only is in the afternoon after a full day of sun. Sunil sat up next to a metal dustbin. He **definitely** wasn't in the right place.

'I said, "I'm going to hit you!"'

A girl walked past, head down, carrying a heavy satchel. A large boy who reminded Sunil a bit of Adam was catching up with her.

'Leave her alone,' Sunil muttered.

He felt groggy from the landing. He got up. He'd seen

places like this in films. A wide

street. All the houses had steps

leading up to a front porch and

those strange mailboxes out front. Telegraph wires crossed the sky like graph paper.

The girl was further down the street and the boy caught up with her, attempting to grab her bag. Sunil heard him call her something. A nasty slur.[1]

'**Stop!**' Sunil shouted. He ran after them.

The boy spun round.

1. A slur is an insulting word which is used to show disrespect for a whole category of people, like people who belong to a particular race or religion.

'Or what?' The boy looked shocked. 'What are you?'

Sunil ignored the question. 'Why are you picking on girls?'

'I don't see no girl. She's one of **them**,' the boy said. He looked again at Sunil, balling his fists. 'And so are you.'

Sunil raised his hands, ready for the punch.

'**Hey**,' the girl said. 'He's just a kid!'

The boy's face was red with anger. He turned on his heel and

faced the girl, his fist pulled back.
'Fine. I'll punch **you!**'

The girl had dropped her satchel
and picked up a piece of brick
from the side of the road. She held
back as if to throw it at the boy. He
paused.

She calmly held his gaze. 'Try it.'

'**No!**' Sunil stepped in between
them.

For a second Sunil thought he
was going to get knocked out. But
then the boy gave a nervous laugh

and moved past them, knocking
into Sunil as he went.

'I wasn't *really* going to hit him!'
the girl said crossly, tossing the
brick back into the gutter.

'I didn't want you to get into
trouble,' Sunil said, rubbing his
shoulder.

'Maybe they would stop bullying
me if I fought back,' said the girl.

'Hitting him won't help,' Sunil
said sagely.

'I wasn't going to,' she said.

Sunil gave a look of disbelief.

'I'm not stupid. If I hurt him, no one would care that he threatened me first,' she said.

Sunil thought she was being dramatic. 'Why was he mad at you?' he asked.

'He missed the school bus. He's not used to having to walk,' said the girl, shrugging.

'But why pick on you?' Sunil asked. 'Did you miss it too?'

She laughed. 'We don't have school buses.'

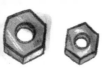

Sunil realised what she meant. He felt a bit foolish. 'Oh. You mean they're only for white people?' he said.

'Yup,' she said.[2]

2. Before 1964, when the US government changed things, there were laws in some states in the USA (known as 'Jim Crow laws') to keep Black and white people from mixing. This was called 'segregation' and was deeply unfair. It meant Black children couldn't go to the same schools as white children. You weren't allowed to use the same hospital if you were sick, or eat in the same room in a restaurant, or drink from the same water fountain.

'Sorry. I'm not from round here; I didn't know,' he said, feeling embarrassed.

'That's alright,' she said holding out her hand. 'I'm Rosa.'[3]

'I'm Sunil,' he said, with one eye still on the boy in the distance.

3. Rosa Parks (1913-2005) was a leader in the civil rights movement (the struggle to get equal rights, particularly for Black people). As an adult she wrote about how she had to defend herself as a child from a white boy bullying her. The only way she could get rid of him was by threatening to hit him with a brick (it isn't mentioned whether there was a time traveller from Manchester with her at the time). When her grandparents found out they punished her for it.

Rosa looked at Sunil's angry expression and laughed. 'Now who wants to beat him up?'

'I heard what he called you,' Sunil said, gritting his teeth.

'Even if you beat him in a fight, you wouldn't change his mind.'

Rosa sighed. 'And he'd take it out on other innocent people.'[4]

'Can't we tell his parents?' asked Sunil.

4. In the USA at this period there were often mobs of white people who accused Black people of crimes against white people. They were very violent and it all happened very publicly. It was terrifying for families like Rosa's. How could you protest against poor treatment when all it took was for a white person to accuse you of looking at them the wrong way for you and your family to be attacked and even killed?

'His parents are worse than he is,' she said. 'Where do you think he learnt those words from?' said Rosa.

'So, we do nothing?' Sunil asked.

'We stood up for ourselves,' Rosa said. 'My family will think that's bad enough.'

'But your family are African American too, aren't they? Surely they want you to fight for equal rights?' said Sunil.

She laughed. 'Not if it sends angry white folks to our house!'

'Yeah, I didn't think of that,' Sunil said.

'When I grow up, I will only follow rules that white people have to follow. I'm using their water fountains, their entrances, I'm getting on their buses...'[5]

5. In 1955, when Rosa Parks was grown up, she was told to stand up on a crowded bus so that white people could sit down. She refused and was arrested. Lots of people had protested the unfair laws in this way, but it was Rosa's story which sparked a boycott of the buses and a debate that eventually saw the law changed.

'Isn't that dangerous?' Sunil asked.

'I would rather die than see people mistreated and be silent about it,' Rosa said. She hoicked her satchel onto her shoulder. 'It is getting late. I hope to bump into you later, Sunil!'

Rosa had only gone a few yards down the road when she thought to ask Sunil if he wanted to come for dinner, but when she turned to ask him, he'd **vanished**.

Chapter Five

Sunil landed back on Alex's roof with a **thump**. He felt sick. Usually, he had some warning before he was transported back to the present. This time his timeline hadn't tugged on his belly button the way it normally did – it had found him instantly. The first tug and he was launched up, super-fast, into the present day.

'Sunil?' Alex popped her head out of the skylight. She sounded angry. 'You could have **died!**'

'How come I didn't feel my timeline?' Sunil asked, confused. He touched his belly button.

'I had to reboot the BM. You got yanked back instantly.' Alex glowered at him. 'Get inside.'

Sunil followed her down the ladder and stairs, back into the living room. The silence was broken only by a **glug** from the lobster tank and the *whirr* of the Boring Machine as it powered back up.

Sunil went over to stroke Wiki who was still crouched on top of Tara's tennis ball. Wiki gave a low growl as Sunil reached for him, then pecked hard at Sunil's finger.

'**Ow!**' Sunil said. 'Why is Wiki here?'

Alex ignored him. 'You've damaged the fence.'

'I didn't go near the fence,' he said, sucking his finger.

'You dropped a ladder on it,' Alex said. 'Didn't you think of securing it to anything? Didn't you think at all?'

'I knew you wouldn't let me use the BM,' Sunil explained.

'So you'd thought you'd **break** your **spine** as revenge?!' said Alex.

'No, but...' Sunil said.

'Do you have any idea of the paperwork I'd have to fill in if you'd fallen?' she said.

'I didn't fall...' Sunil thought a moment. 'And you were the one who was dangerous.'

'Me?!'

'You turned off the Boring
Machine without warning. If I'd
have been inside, my timeline
would have **dragged** me through the
ceiling!'

Alex opened and closed her
mouth a few times. Sunil smirked.
She hadn't thought of that.

Alex readjusted the goggles on
her head. 'So, uh, I take it you didn't
end up at lunchtime?'

'I was in America,' said Sunil.

Alex nodded sagely. 'The 1920s?'

'Yeah, how did you know?' Sunil frowned. 'I gave BM my hoodie. That's not American.'

'It's because I accidentally put some vintage baseball cards in the wrong drawer last week,' Alex confided and, opening the door to the Boring Machine, sat on the downstairs loo.

'Baseball cards?'

'I wanted to use them as a boring object to power the Boring

Machine but I put them in the artefact draw, not the boring draw!' She pointed between the two draws on the machine. 'Somehow one slipped, got caught in the mechanism and the BM got all interested and won't let it go. How was I supposed to know baseball cards aren't boring?'

'Are those like football stickers?'

She nodded. 'One is still stuck the mechanism. So every time I travel to a time between 1900 and

now, I get sent to America near someone's boring collection.'

'Can't you get it out?' Sunil asked, realising he wasn't going to be able to go back to lunchtime if the BM was broken.

'It'll work its way out eventually,' Alex said.

'But I'm missing cricket practice!' Sunil whined. 'I wanted to change what happened today...'

'It's only cricket,' Alex said.

Sunil sighed. She didn't understand. If he wasn't playing for the team now, there was even less chance of him being able to play for an under 19s team one day, and then there was no hope of him ever being a professional.

Alex looked at the despair on his face and slapped her legs. 'I'll have a tinker,' she said.

She took out her toolbox and opened the side panel of the Boring Machine. 'While I look at this,

perhaps you can try and work out what is wrong with Wiki? Mr Shaykes dropped him off this morning and told me to fix him.'

'Why didn't he take him to the vet?' asked Sunil.

'He's not sick; just being weird. He attacked Mr Shaykes while he was making breakfast,' she said, shrugging. 'Mr Shaykes has been much nicer lately, helping me find old objects to test.'

'Like baseball cards?' Sunil asked, wryly. He didn't believe

Mr Shaykes could ever do good –
after all, he had once tried to turn
Sunil into a milkshake. It wouldn't
surprise him if Mr Shaykes hadn't
trained Wiki to be an attack kiwi
instead of a trained fact snuffler.

Sunil approached the fluffy kiwi
who was perched on the tennis ball
he'd thrown earlier. Wiki growled
as he approached.

'Are you ok?' Sunil asked gently.

Wiki snarled and jumped off
the tennis ball. Sunil backed off but

the kiwi chased him around the coffee table, trying to claw at Sunil's trainers with his feet.

'If you're going to be like that, I'm taking my ball back!' Sunil snapped, picking it up.

Wiki immediately changed,

peeping pleadingly and rubbing his beak against Sunil's ankles.

'No!' Sunil said sternly and went back to the Boring Machine. 'Any luck?' he asked Alex.

'Nope, it's still jammed.' Alex handed him his hoodie which he put back on. 'I think if I travel back really far, it might loosen up. Stretch its legs a bit,' she said.

Sunil perked up. 'Can we see dinosaurs?'

'Not that far!' Alex said. 'I've tried going back using a piece of flint before now, and ended up in a swamp surrounded by a group of hungry baryonyx.'[1]

Sunil's eyes widened.

'Fortunately, the Boring Machine couldn't hold me that far back for more than a second or two,

1. Baryonyx is a two-legged dinosaur from the Cretaceous period (145–66 million years ago). Its name means 'heavy claw' and it is likely that it lived near water. It probably ate fish and other dinosaurs – and maybe time travellers if it could get hold of one.

so I was catapulted home before I could scream,' she said.

'You've seen dinosaurs!' exclaimed Sunil.

'We've all seen dinosaurs,' Alex said, shrugging. 'Wiki is technically a dinosaur.[2] To fix the machine we only need to travel a few hundred years or so...'

2. Birds evolved during the Jurassic period (165 million years ago). They are cousins of dinosaurs like T. Rex and share a common ancestor. They survived the extinction event 65 million years ago which killed the other dinosaurs.

She began searching the shelves on her walls, grabbing boxes and shaking their contents out onto the sofa.

'The oldest thing I've got is a broken ceramic bowl… it's probably 12th century.' Alex licked the bowl, thoughtfully. 'It's from somewhere in central Asia… We'll need to wear our Talk Torc translators.'

She handed Sunil a thick metal necklace that reminded him of a pair of chunky headphones.

He'd used one of these before. It was another of Alex's inventions and worked like noise cancelling headphones. It translated any language for both the wearer and whoever they were speaking to so they could understand each other. He put it on, gripped the handles of the Boring Machine and slowly breathed out. With a massive **jolt** he was thrown back in time.

Chapter Six

'Don't move!'

Sunil sat up. A rat skittered away from where he had landed in thick grass. The sun shone above a vast landscape of forested hills and wide-open plains.

'I said don't move.' A boy marched over to Sunil. 'I could have got him!'

'Hi,' Sunil said.

'I'm Temüjin,' the boy said.

'I'm Sunil,' Sunil said, getting up.

Temüjin was dressed in tatty clothes that he was slightly too large for. On his head he had a fur hat and he was carrying a curvy bow that reminded Sunil of a twirly moustache.[1] Under one arm was a dead bird and two large rats tied together in a bundle. Presumably the results of his hunt.

1. Mongol bows are part of the reason why no one could defeat their armies. Their 'recurve' design meant they were very powerful so Mongolian soldiers could shoot long distances and their arrows could pierce armour.

'Did they take your horse?'
Temüjin asked.

'I don't have a horse,' Sunil said.
'Who are "they"?'

'The people who took your
mother.'

'You mean Alex?' Sunil turned
around, scanning the horizon.
'Why would anyone take her?'

'For a wife.' Temüjin stared
at him suspiciously. 'Who's your
father?'

'I don't think you know him,'

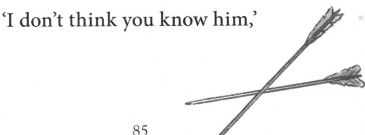

Sunil said, smiling.

Temüjin looked shocked at this.

'Why? Isn't he a warrior?'

'He's an accountant,' said Sunil.

Temüjin shook his head and looked down at the ground. 'You must have hit your head when you fell. Strange, I don't see horse tracks... or any tracks.'

'I'm having a really bad day, so I would be grateful if you could help me find my friend,' said Sunil.

'I saw a group surrounding a stranger by the forest.' Temüjin pointed to a hill topped with trees.

'Can we stop them?' asked Sunil.

Temüjin raised his eyebrows; there was a little smile playing on his lips. 'You are going to fight for her?' he said.

Sunil shrugged. 'If I have to.'

Temüjin grinned. 'Here. I will show you where I saw them.'

The boys walked together up to the hill. The immense size of the lush green steppe made Sunil feel very small. It didn't feel like a real place. It felt like he'd been shrunk down to the size of a beetle and shown a grassy field back home. It was vast.

'See there is my family gerr,' Temüjin said, pointing to two round tents in the distance.[2] His arm swept across to point to another encampment about a kilometre from the tents. 'There is the rest of my father's tribe who abandoned us. They took our animals so it is a

2. A gerr, also known as a yurt, is a traditional Mongolian tent. The Mongolian people were nomadic — they went from place to place, rather than staying in one location and farming.

struggle to keep up when they move on.'[3]

'Why did they abandon you?' asked Sunil.

Temüjin sighed. 'My father had many enemies. One was Temüjin, who I was named after.'

3. The Mongolians prized horses. They showed how rich you were and were also key to survival on the grassland of Mongolia. Children would learn to ride them as toddlers. Mongolian people were such skilled riders that they could fire arrows perfectly while on horseback. They would also train their horses to follow them like dogs.

'He named you after his enemy?' said Sunil, surprised.

'Of course. He killed Temüjin so named me after him. Why, who are you named after?'

Sunil shrugged. 'I think Mum just liked the name.'

Temüjin looked suspiciously at Sunil again but carried on with his story. 'My father took me to live with my bride's family.'

'How old are you?' asked Sunil.

'Nine summers,' said Temüjin.

'You're nine years old and you have a wife!?'

'We're not married yet. Her name is Borte. I had begun working for her family when my brother sent word that my father had been poisoned by the family of his enemy. It was revenge for his enemy's death.'

While he was talking, Temüjin kept looking down, examining the dusty footpath they were on like he had lost something.

'Your dad was **poisoned**?' Sunil said horrified. 'Is he alright?'

Temüjin looked up, confused. 'If he were alive, I would still be with my tribe and not forced to hunt rats,' he said.

'Just because your dad died you were left behind? What about your mum?' asked Sunil.

'Her too,' Temüjin said, in a

matter-of-fact way. 'An old man tried to reason with them, but they killed him.'[4]

'That's terrible,' Sunil said.

---

4. After Temüjin's father was poisoned the rest of their tribe abandoned him and his family. It is only thanks to the hard work of his mother, Hoelun, that they managed to survive. Later, Temüjin formed alliances with other families, but he also secured his position as head of his own family by murdering his older half-brother. Charming!

'Look there!' Temüjin said, pointing at the ground. 'Several horses have been this way recently. This bush is still weeping sap.'

Sunil looked at the fresh green of the broken stem of the plant. 'You can tell just from that?' he said.

'And the hoof marks, here, and there in the mud. She was taken from here,' Temüjin said. 'You can see the horse tracks slow, and circle around some strange footprints.'

'I'm sorry about your dad,' Sunil said, unable to recognise anything other than churned up mud.

Temüjin's eyebrows raised again. 'Why?'

'Can you tell which way they took Alex?' Sunil asked.

'You can see, after they caught her, she walked with them. These are the footprints,' Temüjin said.

Sure enough, Sunil saw a modern looking boot print next to a muddy patch.

'Will they hurt her?' he asked.

'She was walking with them, so they didn't force her or carry her,' said Temüjin.

Sunil didn't like the sound of any of these people. He found Temüjin's explanations chilling. He trotted behind him, agreeing nervously with everything the boy said.

'Who are they?' Sunil asked.

'Warriors. You are not under protection of the Khan so...' he stopped.[5] 'Where did she go?'

5. Even though Mongolian tribes were nomadic they were still organised. Powerful families with many horses, connections, and warriors would protect less powerful tribes and families from those who wanted to steal their horses and food, or kidnap women and children. In return, families would share their wealth with the Khan (the leader) and give him gifts. If you weren't allied to a Khan, you had no protection, and anyone could take your things or even try to kill you.

CHAPTER SEVEN

They were at the edge of the forest.

The path opened out into a clearing.

On one side was a steep drop down

a grassy hillside. Temüjin pointed at

the floor. 'Her footprints are gone.'

Sunil looked but only saw mud.

'Look, she stepped here,'
Temüjin said, pointing at the
ground, 'and here she vanishes, and
all the horses back away.'

Sunil felt a tug on his belly
button and realised what must have
happened. The Boring Machine
was using the power of boredom to
keep them in the past. Alex must
have got too excited from being
kidnapped so her timeline had
found her and pulled her back to

the present. Sunil was about to ask
Temüjin where the warriors had
gone when he felt the boy duck
down next to him.

'**Wolf!**' Temüjin said, pointing
along the path towards the trees in
the distance.

'Where?!' Sunil's belly button
tugged.

'**Shhh…**' Temüjin said.

'Will it eat us?' asked Sunil.

'The wolves don't hunt us. Not
unless…'

'Unless what?' Sunil's heart pounded like he'd been running.

'It is rabid,' said Temüjin.[1]

---

1. Rabies is a deadly disease that swells the brain and can cause the infected person or animal to act strangely and aggressively. It can make them afraid of water and sometimes causes them to drool or froth at the mouth. Once symptoms start it is still impossible to cure, but these days we have a vaccine that can stop you from getting infected, and can treat the disease before you get sick. It's extremely rare in the UK — no one has died of rabies caught here since 1922. It is spread when someone is scratched by an infected animal so if you're in a country where rabies is common then you should see a doctor if you get bitten or scratched.

Sunil scanned the tree line. His heart leapt when he saw something move.

'You see it?' Temüjin raised his bow.

The wolf slunk out of the grass and onto the path. It wasn't much bigger than Sunil's dog Tara but it looked as much unlike Tara as it was possible to look: rake thin with matted fur.

'Can you shoot it?' Sunil asked.

'I only have three arrows,' Temüjin said.

The wolf was still quite far away, walking determinedly. Then it **growled**. Sunil yelped, stepping back. There was something about its shape and the way it moved. All the fairy tales about the big bad wolf never struck him as scary, but this wolf was the most frightening thing Sunil had ever seen. Its nose was pulled right back in a snarl, baring its teeth. White saliva frothed and hung like a gooey shawl from its mouth. The closer it got, the less Sunil felt able to move. He couldn't even feel the tug of his timeline. He only felt one thing: a primal fear.[2]

'**Ahhh!**' Sunil gasped.

Temüjin fired an arrow. It whistled past the target and the wolf started to run at them. Temüjin only had two arrows left.

2. Wolves are dangerous wild animals but rarely attack humans, and usually only do so because they have rabies which changes their behaviour. Humans kill far more wolves every year than wolves kill people.

'Be quiet, I need silence!'
Temüjin snapped at Sunil.

Sunil reeled back as the wolf
barrelled towards them. His arm
brushed the pocket of his hoodie
and he felt Tara's tennis ball there.

Temüjin fired his second arrow
but, once again, he missed.

Sunil grasped the ball in his
pocket and then stepped back
towards Temüjin. His foot planted,
his free arm rose with his leg, and
he held the tennis ball by his eye,

targeting the wolf. The movement was automatic. His weight shifted forward onto his front leg as his bowling arm extended and swung over his shoulder in an arc, releasing the ball at the highest point.

The ball hit the dusty path like an asteroid at the feet of the advancing beast. Small stones hit the wolf at the same time as the tennis ball **bounced** off its nose and ricocheted down the hill. The wolf

stopped, blinking dust from its eyes
as it looked to see what had struck
it. It snarled and launched itself
after the ball. Both ball and wolf
bounced down the steep hillside.

'Run,' Temüjin said, pointing into the woods.

Sunil didn't need telling twice. The pull of his belly button was growing stronger as he ran after the

boy, branches hitting him in the face and twigs snapping underfoot. He thought his timeline was bound to find him any second. Temüjin reached a stream, and each boy jumped over. Sunil landed, gasping and sat down on the muddy bank.

'Our smell will be harder to follow now,' Temüjin said, out of breath. 'What's wrong with your face?'

Tears of relief welled up in
Sunil's eyes.

'Nothing's wrong with it,' he
said.

'You're **weeping!**' said Temüjin.

'I'm happy!' Sunil explained.
'The wolf chased the ball. Did
you see it hit his nose? He was so
confused!'

Temüjin's eyes narrowed. 'I've
never seen anyone throw like that
before.'

'It's called bowling,' Sunil said.

'Who are you?' Temüjin bent over Sunil to look in his eyes. 'You smell like nothing around here.[3] You fell off a horse that left no prints and you defeated a wolf with a **yellow fire ball**.'

3. Traditionally, Mongolians believed that your smell was part of your spirit. The story goes that when Temüjin's mother Hoelun was younger, she was travelling with her fiancé to meet his family. They saw warriors approaching. She gave her fiancé her coat for him to remember her smell by, and told him to flee for his life. They never saw each other again. Instead Hoelun was captured by Yesugei who was Temüjin's father and she ended up marrying him instead.

'I know it looks weird,' Sunil admitted.

Temüjin raised his bow at Sunil. 'You were kind to me,' he said.

'So you're going to **shoot** me?' Sunil held his hands up. He suddenly felt his timeline again, pulling him to his feet. 'How does that make sense?'

'You aren't from here. You can't even follow tracks. Your father isn't a warrior. You are stupid and you cry like an infant.'

'It shouldn't matter who my dad is! Not knowing stuff doesn't make me stupid,' Sunil said angrily. 'And crying stops your eyes from getting dusty!'

'You should never show weakness!' Temüjin barked. 'The man who was kind to my family was killed for it.'

'Standing up for you was brave!' Sunil shouted.

'Your logic is backwards,' Temüjin said, pulling back on his

bow. 'You don't belong here.'

Sunil instantly felt the tug on his belly button as Temüjin released his final arrow. Something hit Sunil hard in the foot as he was catapulted upwards into the sky. The colours blurred and he flipped into the present day.

Chapter Eight

Sunil landed next to Alex on her roof. He sat up and looked at his left foot. There was an arrow sticking out of it. He felt a wave of sick panic and reached for it, only to find that the arrow had pierced through the squishy heel of his trainer.

Alex made a weird gurgling noise. 'Sunil! Your arrow! I mean your foot!'

'It's ok,' Sunil said.

He took his shoe off to show her. The arrow was jammed in, and he couldn't pull it out. He handed it to Alex who examined it closely.

'Where were you?' she asked.

'Tracking you, with a boy called Temüjin. We were attacked by a **wolf!**'

Alex gave up looking at the arrow and Sunil followed her

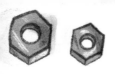

through the skylight and down the ladder.

'You weren't bitten, were you?' she asked.

She placed his shoe in a clamp attached to the coffee table. Wiki ran up to Sunil, **peeping** for the ball.

'No. I bowled Tara's tennis ball towards it. It chased the ball instead of us.' Sunil shook his head at Wiki. 'Then Temüjin tried to kill me.'

'Charming,' Alex said. Using her foot to brace against the coffee table she pulled the arrow out from

the shoe. Panting, she handed Sunil his shoe back and tested the sharp point of the arrow with her finger. 'Are you sure his name was Temüjin?'

'Yeah,' Sunil said.

Alex scanned the bookshelves, pulled out a book and settled down on the sofa next to Wiki who growled and started sniffing around as though looking for something.

Alex squealed. Her finger stabbed a page in the book. 'You met Genghis Khan!' she said.

'No, he was called Temüjin not Genghis.'

'That was his name as a boy!" Alex said.[1]

'Wasn't he like, an emperor or something?' asked Sunil.

---

1. Temüjin changed his name in 1206 to Genghis Khan and there is a lot of debate as to what it actually means. Khan means leader, and Genghis could mean anything from 'strength' to 'ocean'. The idea is that at the time the Mongols believed all the land on earth was in one block and surrounded by ocean, so Genghis Khan, Ocean Ruler, was inescapable, he encircled everywhere you could go.

'He was more than an emperor; he was one of the most successful military leaders in history.'[2]

Sunil looked sceptical. 'Are you sure it was him? This boy was hunting rats. To eat,' he said.

---

2. During Genghis Khan's reign the Mongols conquered the largest land empire in history (that is the largest empire when all the land was joined together rather than overseas). Many historians think that if they hadn't had a leadership crisis when Genghis Khan died, they could have easily have conquered the whole of Europe.

'He grew up an outcast,' Alex said. 'Genghis Khan was incredibly smart and ruthless.'

'He was **nuts**,' Sunil said. 'He thought helping people was bad…'

'It was a different time on the steppe,' Alex explained. 'Loyalty to your own family and Khan was everything. But Genghis was different. He promoted people who didn't have a birthright to power. He made people generals on merit…'

'He didn't reward me on merit!' said Sunil.

'Well, perhaps you taught him a lesson.' Alex went over to the boring machine. 'Hey, it worked! I can see the corner of the stuck baseball card; can you fetch me some tweezers?'

Sunil began searching through the objects on the sofa.

'I can't find any!' Sunil said.

'Ask Wiki; he's got a long beak,' Alex suggested.

The kiwi fluffed himself up and **growled** as Sunil approached.

'I'm sorry I lost your ball. I'll get you another, ok?' Sunil said.

Wiki **huffed**.

'Please can you come and help?' Sunil asked. 'If we can get the baseball card out then I'll be able to travel back to this lunchtime, not take my maths test and

then none of this bad stuff will happen.'

The bird relented and let Sunil carefully pick him up. Alex and Sunil watched as Wiki reached into the Boring Machine's gears to pull at the corner of the stuck baseball card.

'`That tickles`,' the BM giggled.

'It's still stuck,' Alex said, frowning. 'But I reckon one more trip and it'll be loose enough to pull out!'

'You mean we can travel back again?' Sunil asked hopefully.

'As long as we go back far enough.' Alex went over to the sofa and held up a strange metal pendant. 'This pomander is from Tudor times.'[3]

3. A pomander was a metal or cloth bag. Tudors would stuff them full of herbs and hold them by their noses to disguise the foul stench of other Tudors. We have an idea that Tudors were smelly, but really that is only the fact that most places had open sewers and used home-made chemicals

'Tudors?' Sunil raised his eyebrows. 'I think we did them at school. Is that Shakespeare?'

'That's right, during Elizabeth I's reign,' Alex said, putting the pomander in the BM's drawer. 'And it was Queen Mary I before her, and

for cleaning and building which included ingredients like horse urine. The Tudors might not have had baths, but they did wash themselves. They'd use wet, warm cloth or dry clean linen to remove dirt and smells. It was important to smell nice, as they thought bad smells caused illness.

Edward VI before her, and Henrys VII and VIII before him.'

'Lots of them then?' said Sunil.

'Come on!' Alex said.

Alex was so intent on travelling, she only noticed that Sunil was still holding Wiki the kiwi at the last second when he had already grabbed the handle to the Boring Machine.

CHAPTER NINE

Sunil landed by a hedge. He turned
around and was confronted with
more hedge. It was neatly trimmed,
over two metres tall and at one end
he glimpsed a large lawn and some
flowerbeds. There was a strange
'**thump**' noise every now and then,
followed by clapping.

A girl about Sunil's age turned the far corner and stopped in her tracks. She was wearing a strange dress with puffed sleeves and a collar which came right up under her chin. She had white cap like a bonnet on her head which did nothing to disguise her bright orange hair.

'Have you seen my friend Alex?' he asked as her dark eyes looked him up and down. 'Or a kiwi?'

'You must address me, as My Lady Elizabeth,' she said. 'If you are a sultan's son, I think you should know that I've vowed to refuse all proposals.'[1]

'Okay,' Sunil said.

1. At this time Henry VIII (Elizabeth's father) had angered the Pope and the Catholic parts of Europe by setting up his own church. They refused to trade with him, so he made friends with the Muslim people in Turkey and North Africa and traded with them instead. This is probably why Elizabeth assumes Sunil is the son of a sultan.

'Aren't you going to ask me why?' she asked.

'I wasn't.' Sunil attempted to walk past her but she stepped into his path.

'My Lady Elizabeth,' she prompted.

'I wasn't, My Lady Elizabeth,' Sunil repeated, moving round her and walking towards the end of the hedges.

'How should I address you?' she said, trotting along beside him.

'Just Sunil,' he said. 'I need to find Alex and Wiki.'

He walked towards the formal garden where the lawn gave way to a knee-high hedge that formed geometric zig zags around harshly clipped trees. Surrounding them was a high red brick wall and an enormous building with tens of dark windows looming over them. Again, he heard the strange '**thump**' sound and clapping.

'What is that noise?' Sunil asked.

'My father, the king, is hosting an archery contest,' Elizabeth said as another **thump** and round of clapping began. 'I'm supposed to be watching.'[2]

2. Archery was very important in mediaeval and Tudor times. Henry VIII made it law that every man had to have longbows for himself, his servants and his children. He ordered that people practise shooting on their holidays just in case they were needed for war. Women also learned to shoot arrows but for sport and hunting, not battle.

'If your dad is the king, why are you My Lady Elizabeth and not Princess Elizabeth?'

She sighed. 'Because my parents weren't married. I mean, they thought they were at the time, but according to my father and a lot of lawyers, that marriage didn't count.'

'That's weird,' said Sunil.

'Not really. My older sister Mary isn't a princess either because my father's first marriage also didn't count.'[3]

'How come your parents' marriage didn't count?' Sunil asked.

3. Elizabeth's father, Henry VIII, was married to his first wife, Catherine of Aragon, for twenty years but they only had one child together – Elizabeth's older sister Mary. Henry was desperate to have a son who could become king after him, so he claimed that it wasn't a proper marriage because Catherine had previously been married to his older brother Arthur (who died when he was only 15). The Pope refused to let Henry marry someone else; Catherine was from Spain and the Spanish Royal family put pressure on the Pope to keep their daughter married to the King of England.

'Because my mother had bewitched him to leave his first wife... or she committed treason or something,' Elizabeth said, plucking at the plants. 'So, he had her executed...'[4]

'What?!'

'I was only a toddler; I don't

---

4. Henry VIII was upset with Anne Boleyn (Elizabeth's mother) for not having a son. She was also unpopular in court with his friends and advisors as she would offer her opinions on matters of state. So they accused her of having multiple affairs. They even suggested she used witchcraft to cast love spells on the king, tricking him into marrying her.

remember.' She shrugged. 'Then he married my mother's lady-in-waiting, Jane Seymour, who died after my brother Edward was born. I don't remember her either.'

'So your dad has been married three times?' asked Sunil.

She was given a trial and she and all the unpopular men in the court she was accused of cheating on the king with, INCLUDING HER OWN BROTHER, were sentenced to death. We know the trial was unfair as Henry had requested that the executioner come from France... before the trial had even begun!

'No, five. He split up with Anne of Cleves and married my cousin about two years ago…' She tailed off and looked sad. 'She was executed before Easter.'[5]

5. Anne of Cleves was from a protestant area of Germany. Unlike Henry's other wives, he hadn't fallen in love with her first; he married her because he thought it would be useful to have her brother's help if a lot of Catholic countries like France and Spain tried to invade England (the Pope was still upset with Henry for divorcing Catherine of Aragon). The marriage only lasted a few months though. Catherine Howard, Henry's fifth wife was Elizabeth's cousin. She was much younger than Henry (only a teenager) and had an affair with a boy her own age. When the king found

'He **killed** her?!' Sunil exclaimed.

'Chopped off her head...' She put her hands around her throat. 'Which is why I'm never getting married. My father has been married five times and half of his wives have been beheaded.'

out he had her beheaded. She was the first of Henry's wives to make an effort to include Elizabeth so it must have been very upsetting. Henry went on to have one more wife – Catherine Parr – but he died before she did. She must have been quite relieved!

'Not half,' Sunil corrected her, remembering her story. 'Two out of five.'

'So only a two-fifths chance of having my head cut off?' Elizabeth said. 'No thank you.'

Sunil suddenly thought of the maths test. It was obvious. ⅖... two

out of five! Of course that was a smaller fraction than ½… one out of two. It made sense.

'If you wait until you are queen, then no one can cut your head off,' said Sunil.

Elizabeth laughed. 'I'm not going to be queen!'

Sunil cocked his head. He was sure Alex had said there was a Queen Elizabeth I. 'How come?'

'Firstly, my younger brother Edward will be king. He's a boy so is first in line.'[6]

6. Edward VI became king when Henry VIII died in 1547. He was only nine years old! He died when he was just fifteen. Despite his short reign he did have a massive impact on the everyday lives of his people. Edward changed lots of things, like banning Catholic mass. He also allowed priests and vicars to get married. He tried to make sure England stayed Protestant by naming Lady Jane Grey as his successor. It didn't work though. She only lasted 9 days on the throne, and then was executed within a year on the orders of Edward's older sister, Mary. Mary was Catholic and undid all of Edward's reforms.

'Yeah,' Sunil said, remembering what Alex had said. 'But then, after him.'

'He'll grow up and have children,' she said. 'And if he doesn't, I'm not a princess. I'm Lady Elizabeth, like you keep forgetting. I'm not in the line of succession. Thirdly, even if I were, and if Edward died without having any children, and the crown passed onto his sisters… my older sister Mary would get it.'

'Mary I,' Sunil nodded.

Elizabeth laughed. 'That's never going to happen.'[7]

'But if she were queen…' Sunil suggested.

'Unlikely…' replied Elizabeth.

'And didn't have kids…' said Sunil.

'But she loves kids. Not me or Edward but…' Elizabeth said.

'And she died?' asked Sunil.

7. Mary I became queen in 1553 after Edward's death. She wasn't able to have children though, which is how Elizabeth ended up becoming queen.

'**Maaaybe?** But that is assuming my dad's older sister's children don't have sons. They are Scottish monarchs... people always prefer boys over girls.'[8]

'Why?'

Elizabeth thought for a moment. 'Good question, I suppose in your case you wouldn't want a woman

8. Elizabeth's cousin, Mary, Queen of Scots, was the centre of many plots against Elizabeth later in her reign. She was seen as more legitimate as she was King Henry VIII's niece and her parents were married. (Elizabeth's had been too, but it had ended... badly).

as sultan. You wouldn't want to be ruled by a sultana would you?"[9]

Sunil laughed at her joke. Before he could say that he couldn't see a raisin why not, they heard **screaming**.

---

9. A sultana can be either the wife of a sultan OR a seedless light brown raisin. Just don't mix them up. It would be a strange wedding.

CHAPTER TEN

'It's coming from the tennis court!'
Elizabeth said.

She turned on her heel and ran
along the side of the enormous
building, skidding on the brick path
as she rounded the corner. Sunil
was amazed at how fast she was in

her long dress. Her red hair fought against her cap as she sprinted towards a door that people were pouring out of in a panic.

'What was that thing?' Sunil heard one of them say.

'It looked like an angry grouse,' said another.

'Don't worry the gentlemen will kill it,' said one of the ladies.

'**Wiki!**' Sunil exclaimed, heading into the building.

He nearly tripped on the
reeds that covered the floor of the
entrance. Elizabeth pushed past
him and ran down a long corridor.
It smelt of roast dinner, fresh
herbs and smoke. Tapestries hung
from the walls and sunlight cast
rainbows through stained glass
windows.

The noise grew louder. Men
were arguing. They held wooden
tennis racquets and looked sweaty.

'It ruined my game!' said one.

'I'm not killing it. It likely escaped the king's menagerie,' said another.[1]

'His menagerie is in the Tower, not here…' someone said.

'Where did it come from?' the first man asked.

'**Ahh!**' Another man barrelled through the door. 'Someone set

---

1. The Tower of London was where the royal family kept their exotic pets. The Tudors kept lions, leopards, an eagle, wolf, tiger, lynx and a porcupine at various times. However they also had pets. Horses and dogs were always popular, (Henry VIII had two beagles called Cut and Ball) and for a time marmosets and small monkeys were fashionable too.

their dog on it!'

'**No!**' Sunil shouted and barged past them. 'Wiki?'

The men stopped arguing to greet Elizabeth as she rushed past them.

'My lady!'

'My dear lady!'

'My dear sweet lady.'

'Let me through! If it belongs to my father, I want to return it to him!' Elizabeth grunted, but they held her back.

Sunil ran into a hall. Numbers were painted on the walls and a bell hung from the awning above him. He walked to the waist-high wall that divided the main room from the viewing area to stare at the strange painted lines and markings on the polished wooden floor.[2] There, in the middle of this unfamiliar court, was Wiki, sitting on a white ball.

2. A game called real tennis was popular with the rich in Europe during Tudor times. It was played indoors, and was very unlike the tennis we are familiar with today. For example, you were allowed to bounce the ball off the walls and could get bonus points for hitting bells and paintings!

'Wiki?' Sunil went to the opening in the gallery wall and ran towards him.

'No, Sunil! Get down!' someone hissed.

It was too late. The kiwi puffed himself up and **shrieked** at Sunil, charging at his shoes. Sunil **yelped** and ran back towards the opening, but Wiki blocked his way, forcing Sunil to climb up onto the wall.

'What's wrong with you?' Sunil shouted down at the fluffed-up bird snapping at his shoe laces.

'Get down here!' the voice hissed again.

It was Alex, she was sitting on the floor on the other side of the wall.

Sunil jumped down next to her. 'What's going on?'

'Wiki ran in here and interrupted a game of tennis. We don't have long; I can feel my timeline,' Alex said. 'Wiki will go first as he's the smallest. We need to get him outside.'

Sunil nodded. If they didn't get outside before their timelines caught up with them, they would fall up and hit the ceiling. He looked over to Wiki who had gone back to sit on his tennis ball.

'Why is he so obsessed with balls?' said Sunil.

Elizabeth had pushed through the men outside. They were still at the doorway while she ducked down out of Wiki's sight and next to Sunil.

'My Lady Elizabeth!' Sunil jumped up. 'This is Alex.'

'Oh **wow**,' Alex said. 'It's an honour to meet you!'

'The gentlemen said it has the temper of a wild boar,' Elizabeth said pointing through the gap in the wall to where Wiki was still growling. 'They want to set dogs on it, but none will agree whose dog to risk. I'm sure my father will be pleased if we can capture it unharmed.'

'I'm surprised you want to please him,' Sunil tutted.

'Sunil!' Alex said. 'Her dad is Henry VIII.'

'I don't care. He **killed** her mum!' said Sunil.

'He was right to. My mother confessed to her crimes,' Elizabeth said sadly.

'Oh, Elizabeth!' Alex squeezed her arm. 'She had to. If she hadn't confessed, or praised your father when she was executed...'

'She praised him?!' Sunil spluttered.

'... you would have been thrown out of the court,' Alex said.

'I don't think this is a healthy family dynamic,' Sunil said.

'You don't think she was **evil?**' Elizabeth asked slowly.

'No! She was protecting you like a good mother would...' Alex paused. '**Oh!**'

'What?' said Sunil.

'Wiki!' Alex replied.

'What about him?' asked Sunil.

'He attacked Mr Shaykes when he was making breakfast. I bet anything Mr Shaykes was having **eggs!**' Alex said.

Sunil looked over to Elizabeth who shrugged.

'He thinks that tennis ball is an **egg!** Wiki's feeling broody!' said Alex.

Chapter Eleven

Just then there was a series of murmurs from outside the tennis court of 'Your Majesty,' 'Your Grace,' 'Your Majesty.' Sunil peeked over the barrier to see a group of men burst through a door on the opposite side of the court. All but one were holding longbows and

arrows. The other, who was by
far the most fancily dressed was
limping. He looked tired and sweaty
and had a short grey beard. His
mouth was too small for his round
face and his voice was too high for
his enormous frame.

'Ah, so that is the **beast!**'
he said, his head
cocked to the side.
'Looks no more than
a puffed-up curlew!'

Wiki jumped off his tennis ball and **growled** at the king.

'Shall I get a cage for it, Majesty?' one of the gentlemen asked timidly.

'No, hand me my bow. Once I dispatch it, get the cook to bake it into a pie,' King Henry said.

Alex immediately grabbed Sunil before he launched himself over the wall to protest. She held Sunil back as he watched the king reach out with his jewelled fingers for a longbow.

'Not much meat on the creature,' Henry said, pulling back the string of his bow.

'You have to stop him!' Sunil pleaded to Elizabeth.

The pull on Sunil's belly button was getting stronger. They hadn't much time left to get Wiki outside before they all flew up and hit the roof.

'Me? He doesn't care what I say!' she said.

They heard the bow release,

with a '**schnook**' sound and then a
rattle as the arrow clattered off the
tennis court wall.

'I need **silence!**' roared the king.
'Who spoke?'

'It was me, Your Majesty!'
Elizabeth popped her head up above
the gallery wall as Sunil was pulled
down by Alex.

'Lady Elizabeth?! What are you
doing here?' asked King Henry.

As Elizabeth answered him,
Alex whispered to Sunil, 'I'll

distract Wiki with the arrow. You get the ball and run for it!'

Sunil darted out from behind the gallery wall and onto the tennis court. Meanwhile Alex made a loud **shushing** noise like a train. Wiki immediately left his tennis ball to attack her. She jumped over the wall and scooped up the arrow, using it like a fencer to keep the kiwi at bay. Sunil ran to the tennis ball. He looked up to see a horrified Henry VIII and bobbed a bow before picking it up. It felt more like a mini cricket ball than a tennis ball.[1]

'Hey, Wiki!' Sunil taunted the kiwi. 'I've got your egg!'

The kiwi stopped attacking Alex and looked round at Sunil. He **shrieked** in outrage and charged.

'**Run!**' Elizabeth said, barrelling towards the door where the king and his gentlemen were standing agog.

'**Make way!** Coming through!'

1. Real tennis balls were made with cork and hand stitched with rags around the outside. This meant they were harder to bounce than modern rubber tennis balls.

Elizabeth yelled. '**Make way** for Lady Elizabeth and the king's kiwi keepers!'

The gentlemen lurched aside as Elizabeth, Sunil (clutching a tennis ball), Wiki (**screaming** like a ghoul in a singing contest), and Alex (tossing the arrow back to the king), all rushed out of the room.

Sunil didn't think it was possible for a bird to be so upset. He almost wanted to stop and hand over the ball, but they had to get outside. His

feet were barely touching the reeds which were strewn on the floor as his timeline pulled him harder and harder.

He followed Elizabeth along the corridor and outside into the sunshine just as the tugging on his belly button pulled him off his feet. He got a brief glimpse of Wiki, still **shrieking**, shooting up into the sky, Alex grinning from ear to ear and Elizabeth, dark eyes wide with surprise. But then he was launched like an arrow, back up to the present day.

CHAPTER TWELVE

When they landed, Wiki jumped on Sunil and raised his claws. Sunil quickly threw the tennis ball down through the skylight. The kiwi barrelled after it.

'Do you think we got Elizabeth into trouble?' Sunil asked.

'Oh, not too much,' Alex said, climbing down the ladder.

'She didn't think she was going to be queen,' said Sunil.

'Well, she was. For forty-five years,' Alex said, helping Sunil down off the ladder.

When they went into the living room, Wiki was already perched happily on his new ball.[1]

'Maybe I should get him a chicken to raise,' Alex said dubiously. She went round to the Boring Machine and exclaimed,

1. In some species of kiwi only the male incubates the egg, in others, both males and females share the role. There are no species of kiwi where only the female keeps the egg warm. Kiwis have enormous eggs for their body size. They are massive — larger than a tennis ball. Other birds lay small eggs because they have to fly, while a female kiwi can produce a large, heavy egg as she doesn't need to worry about being able to take off. Big eggs mean strong, fit chicks, who can walk as soon as they hatch.

'It worked! I can reach the card! Just a second.'

'Ahhhh,' said the Boring Machine. 'That's better.'

Alex and held it up.

'Let me see!' said Sunil.

He took the faded card from Alex and looked closely at the black and white picture. 'George Eggler of the New York Mutuals.' Sunil smiled at the man's large chin.

'Statistically, George Eggler was the worst

`home run hitter of all
time`,' chirped the BM.

'Yes, but home runs were harder
in the nineteenth century than
in the modern game,' Alex said
defensively.

'And at least he got to be a
professional,' Sunil said.

'The Boring Machine is fixed.
We could take you back to this
lunchtime if you like,' Alex said.

Sunil paused for a moment. If he
went back would Rosa have hit that

boy and got into trouble? Would Genghis Khan have been bitten by a rabid wolf? Would Elizabeth still think her mother was evil? Would Alex still not know what was wrong with Wiki? He thought of changing what had happened. But crying in front of Adam or missing cricket practice didn't seem like such a big deal anymore.

'I don't think I want to,' he said.

'Good,' Alex said. 'Because you can't change what has already

happened. Even if you haven't done it yet.'

There was a **knock** on the door. Sunil answered it.

'Sunil! There you are!' Sunil's dad smiled. 'What happened to the fence? Where's Alex?'

'I'm here!' Alex said, closing the door to the BM.

'Why is my ladder on top of the fence between our houses?'

'Erm...' she smiled. 'Must have fallen out of the loft.'

'How…' Sunil's dad shook his head and looked down at Sunil. 'Wow, Sunil you're looking much better!'

'Yeah,' grinned Sunil. 'I've been helping Alex repair the…'

Alex nudged him, reminding him to keep the Boring Machine secret.

'I've been helping her with some experiments,' said Sunil.

'And you're feeling better about your maths test?' asked Sunil's dad.

'Oh yes!' Sunil said. 'I understand fractions, I just needed to think about them differently. I kind of thought that failing one test would mean I would never catch up again. But the truth is, you can never predict what you are going to be in the future.'

'Can't you?' said his dad.

'Did you know Genghis Khan grew up as a poor outcast who ate rats?' asked Sunil.

'Er…' his dad looked confused.

'And Elizabeth I never thought she would be queen...' said Sunil.

'I suppose?' Sunil's dad gave Alex a puzzled look. 'And you're not upset about missing cricket?'

Sunil shrugged. 'I know I can still bowl as well as I ever could.'

'You've had quite the turn around.' His dad ruffled Sunil's hair. 'You should do experiments together more often!'

'Oh, don't worry, we will!' Alex said.

VISIT WWW.BLOOMSBURY.COM FOR MORE BOOKS BY ISZI LAWRENCE.